Apt
10/08

ADH:
6907

SANTA CRUZ CITY-COUNTY LIBRARY SYSTEM

0000119231389

D0601585

JEASY

Segal, John.

Alistair and Kip's great
adventure /
c2008.

SANTA CRUZ PUBLIC LIBRARY

SANTA CRUZ, CALIFORNIA 95060

Alistair and Kip's Great Adventure!

John Segal

MARGARET K. McELDERRY BOOKS
NEW YORK LONDON TORONTO SYDNEY

For Emily and Josh, always

Margaret K. McElderry Books * An imprint of Simon &
Schuster Children's Publishing Division * 1230 Avenue
of the Americas, New York, New York 10020 *
Copyright © 2008 by John Segal * All rights reserved,
including the right of reproduction in whole or in part
in any form. * Book design by Ann Bobco * The text for
this book is set in Blockhead. * The illustrations for this
book are rendered in watercolor. * Manufactured in
China * 1 2 3 4 5 6 7 8 9 10 * Library of Congress
Cataloging-in-Publication Data * Segal, John. * Alistair
and Kip's great adventure / written and illustrated
by John Segal.—1st ed. * p. cm. * Summary: Alistair
and Kip build a boat and soon find themselves sailing
down the creek to the river to the bay and out to sea
where a violent storm threatens to capsize them. *
ISBN-13: 978-1-4169-0280-5 (hardcover) * ISBN-10:
1-4169-0280-5 (hardcover) * [1. Boats and boating—
Fiction. 2. Adventure and adventurers—Fiction. 3.
Whales—Fiction.] I. Title. * PZ7.S45258Alk 2008 *
[E]—dc22 * 2006019870

FIRST
EDITION

It was Tuesday morning.

Alistair was bored.

"Kip, let's do something new!" said Alistair. "We could build a boat and travel to far and distant lands."

"What kind of boat . . .?" asked Kip.

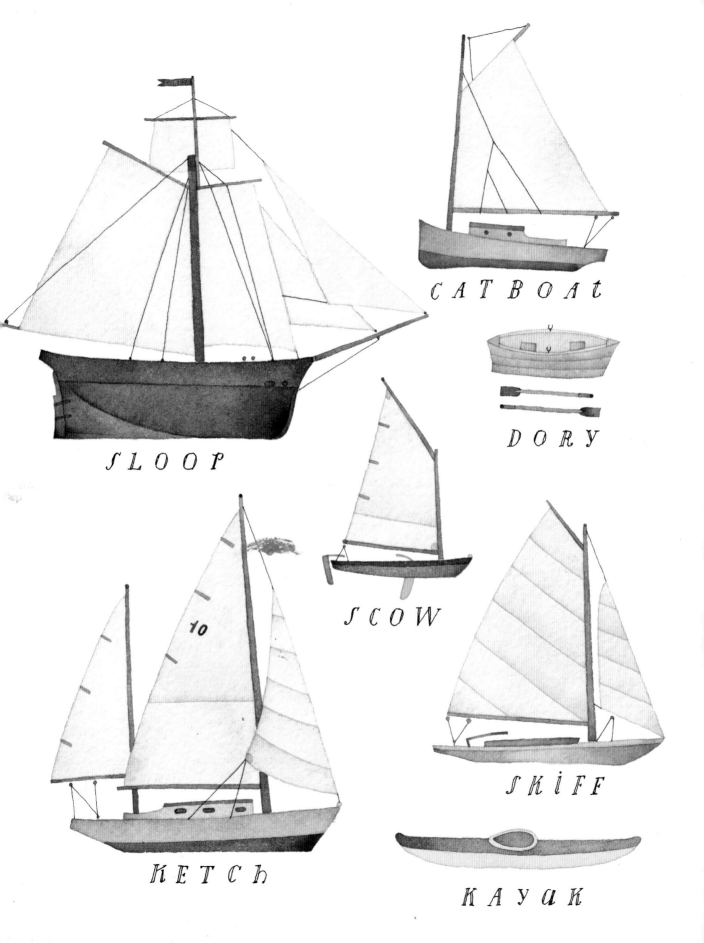

CATBOAT

DORY

SLOOP

SCOW

KETCH

SKiFF

KAYAK

Alistair knew just what to do.

He and Kip gathered wood and paint

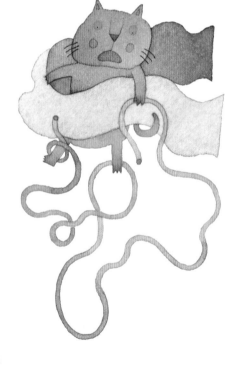

and cloth and rope

and hammer and nails. And then they went to work.

They measured,   cut,

hammered,   and glued.

Before they knew it . . .

. . . their boat was built.

But it was too late.

Alistair had cast off.

The boat was drifting downstream.

"Quick, Kip, jump in!" shouted Alistair.

Their voyage had begun.

They rowed . . .

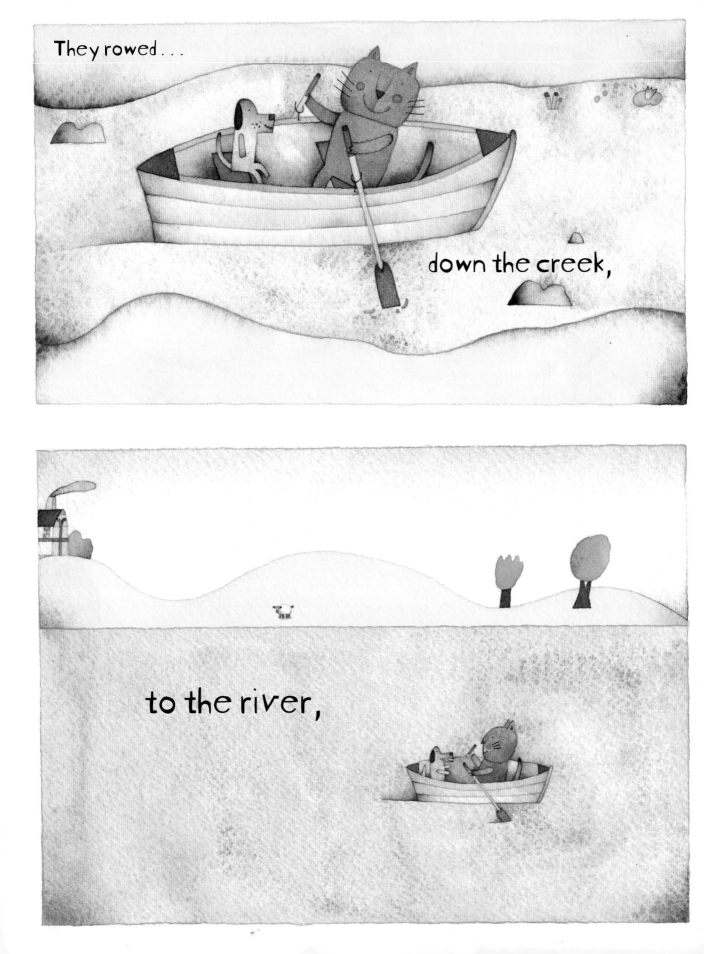

down the creek,

to the river,

into the bay . . .

. . . and out to sea.

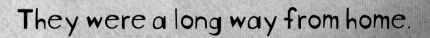

They were a long way from home.

Suddenly a giant wave picked up the boat and hurled it through the air.

Another wave pulled
Alistair and Kip
down deep into the sea.

"Hey, you scared me!"
bellowed the whale.

"Please help us!

We need to get home!"

"Well, why didn't
you say so?
Climb aboard. . . ."

They rode through the bay,

to the river,

and up the creek . . .

. . . all the way home.

"Good-bye
and thank you!"
said Alistair.

"That was **fun**, Kip.

Tomorrow let's build an airplane!"